UNDER THE ACT OF KILLING

HE WAS OFFICIALLY MY UNIVERSE, THAT CONSISTED THE MOON AND THE STARS.

SHIZA MOHAMMED SHAIK

Made with ♥ on the Notion Press Platform
www.notionpress.com

To my Captain..

Contents

Contents

I

Chapter one

"Father, can I go now? My friends must be waiting"

"Stay for longer, I want you to meet the son of the Italian unit. He's a charming being with luscious looks."

I give father a look. I don't want to get married so soon. I don't want to date either. I have dreams to achieve, places to go to... What is my dream? I want to become a pilot, start an airline. Killing was never on my list, never will be. I don't support what my father does, but I definitely don't hate him. I respect him as my father, but never as a person who performs the act of killing for a living. I fear my father, hence I have no choice but to listen to the words that come out of his mouth.

"Yes father." I say politely and bow in front of him. He gives me a smile and taps my shoulder.

Just then there's a grand entrance of another unit walking into the party. The Italian mafia has arrived to Fathers retirement party. I see the darling most praised son of the unit. I must say, I'll agree with father on this one. His curly brown hair goes well with the black suit he has on. He's tall and his brown hazelnut eyes hits the spot.

The family approaches father.

"Congratulations on your retirement, Mr. Marcom White." The head of the Italian unit says.

"Thank you." Father replies with a warm smiles as they shake hands.

Father looks over at me on his right and points to the son with his eyes.

"Navon, this is my daughter, Daphne. Daphne sweetheart, this is Navon Vanchover."

Navon looks at me and grabs my hand. He gives it a soft peck. I force a smile on my face. Navon looks back at me as he lets go of my hand. He gives me a smile. His smile is contagious which causes me to smile wide.

"Why don't the both of you go over the bridge and talk yeah?" Father suggests us to do so.

I nod because fathers orders are the most important for me. Navon and I walk towards the bridge outside. The bridge is covered with flowers, especially pink and purple ones. It's crossing a small lake. We walk towards the bridge. Navon leans over the side with his arms rested on the side of the bridge. Right now, it's just Navon and I with the shine of the night light.

"Well aren't you a beauty. I'm a very lucky man to be declaring you as my wife." Navon says breaking the silence. I can't give this man false hopes. I need to let him know.

"Navon, with all due respect, I must let you know, that I've no intention whatsoever to marry you. I'm just here, following my fathers orders. I have dreams to achieve, places to go and a life to live. So please, here after do not keep any expectations upon our marriage."

I feel cruel for saying all this but I had to and it needed to be done. There's no expression on his face. I'm scared to wits now. Mafias can not be trusted whatsoever in what they can do next.

"Well..." There's a long pause in what he's about to say. I'm afraid he's offended, or feels anger.

"You are an ambitious woman, what do aspire to become in life?" Navon asks with a smile on his face which doesn't seem fake. I think I'm glad he's understanding?

"I aspire to become a captain. Start an airline of my own." I say very enthusiastically. I love talking about my career.

"Really? Well..." *pause* "Nothing."

Strange? What was he going to tell me?

"No tell me." I fold my arms and face him. Now I need to know.

"I could've sworn I overheard our fathers talking about passing the company to you."

My jaw drops and my eyes widen. This can't be. I can't deal with a company that does the wrong acts. I can't go undercover.

"I'm sorry." I say to Navon as I rush towards the inside of the cafe.

I search for father and he's nowhere to be found. I grab a hold of my satin dress and sprint towards his cabin. I bang the door open only to find Navons father strangling my father. I scream and pull father away from him.

I hear loud thumps and realize, the whole unit of Italy has reached to go after Father. How can this be? The Italian unit is not a rivalry unit to us. Navon's father, Romain speaks over the phone in a whole different language to his leaders. It's not Italian, it's French! Our biggest enemies and rivals. The French unit has been after father ever since I had been little. The struggles father had to go through was unbearable to watch.

I see Navon running from behind. He's trying to prevent his father from coming close to us. I still have father in my arms. He's getting breathless, I'm breathing heavily.

My vision gets blurry in panic and all I can see is Navon trying to stop his father. The next thing I know is the French unit shooting guns towards father. **No! NO! NO!**

FATHER I'M HERE!

ꕥ

II

Chapter two

"Why did you try stopping your father? You are our enemies." I ask as we stand on the same bridge in the same cafe it happened.

"Because I'm just like you Daphne." Navon says facing towards me leaning against the ledge. I give him a look of confusion.

"Look we're enemies, we're not supposed to be together but I need to tell you something." I give him a nod as a sign that I'm listening.

"I also don't support my father on what he does. I believe that all of us must be in unity. So, I get you. And ever since your father pass-"

"Don't continue that sentence Navon." I give him a warning and he sighs. I don't want to hear it nor do I want to believe it.

"Daphne, I could leave my father, my unit, my everything just so I could stay with you." He says as tears start to form in his eyes. I stand up straight.

"Your father and his leaders killed my father. No, I don't want to. You stopped your father, but how do I know you regret it? And at what cost? I can never stay with a family like yours. I don't want to. You're my enemy. Always have been. Nothing more than that. How do I know that you weren't just acting? I can't trust you, your father or your unit"

Navon looks speechless. Maybe I went too harsh on him, but I know what I did is for the best.

"I- Daphne please."

He grabs my arm but I push my hand away from him

"You are our enemies! Let's keep it that way." I immidiately leave, refusing to show my tears in front of him. How could he still come after me?

"FINE! Let's keep it that way." Navon screams and I don't dare to look back.

I get a call, "there's a need for you in the office ma'am."

A sense of worry arises in me. I hang up and immidiately get into my car completely leaving Navon to be.

III

Chapter three

I'm in the car. I get continous calls and text messeges from the office. Some are concerning. I'm so worried now. I finally reach the office and I rush inside. I see my assistant and question her about what happened while I was away. She directs me to my cabin.

"It's your mother." She says.

My eyes widen in shock. Why is she here now? What does she want? My Mother? I haven't seen her since the past 10 years ever since she left father for some Russian CEO. To this day, I hate for making father feel like trash.

I go in my cabin and see her waiting. She's sitting on the chair infront of my table with my monitor on it. I take my sunglasses off to see if it actually is her. Holy shit it is. She looks luxury, birkin bag, her usual shit custom made from Versace. She's doing really well, I'm sure the Russian dude is spoiling her well. Before she gets off her phone and notices that I'm here, I clear my throat causing her to turn back. She stares at me for sometime and gives me this evil smile that I've hated. That smile always meant trouble.

She spreads her arms for a hug but I pull myself away and take a seat. I put my stuff down with a stern face.

"What do you want?" Her smile drops.

She takes a seat in front of me, "Daph, I've missed you."

I roll my eyes. I hate and love those words at the same time.

"You didn't." I say

"What do you mean Daph? I'm your mother."

"Exactly, I'm your daughter, yet you still came after abandoning father and I 10 years ago. Do you even know where father is right now?" I say screaming at her.

"Daph, I've been busy. I'm so so sorry for not even contacting the both of you. I know where he is. He's not with us anymore."

"No, do you even care? Why are you even here?" I have anger built in me.

"Well, I, Why else would I be here? I'm here for you."

I don't believe in those words.

"No you're not. I don't want you here. Before you cause any trouble, you need to leave. Thank you for stopping by Maria Jane."

She looks a bit dissapointed but she gets up from her place. Right when she does, she gets a call.

I check the security camera just to make sure she's leaving for good. The security cameras can record voices and noises. I had forgotten about this feature. She kept her phone on speaker. Unintentionally, eavesdropping. I heard her 'Russian guy' saying, "Did you get it?"

"No! I don't think she has that kinda money."

I sigh. I knew it. I knew she wasn't here for me but instead for my money. I knew she never cared for father or for me. She could go screw off for all I care. I call out to my assistant and warn her to never let anyone in without my presence. My assistant nods and leaves the cabin. My cabin gives me so much trauma. I never want anyone else to be here with me. I only get reminded of that incident.

IV

Chapter four

"Show me your finest piece of earrings."

The owner pulls out pearl earrings. It's the most beautiful piece of earrings I've ever witnessed.

"It's made of real pearls worn by the queen of England in the 1900s."

I grab a hold of the earrings.

"It's beautiful. Name the price."

"A million dollars."

I smile as the owner says a million dollars. I could see why it was worth so much. I put the earrings back down on the plate.

"Have it packed."

"Certainly."

The owner smiles. I smile back and patiently wait for my earrings. I press my elbows against the table and look around until I notice a red laser pointed towards me. I panic. Immidiately someone pulls me and drags me to a corner where I'm hidden.

"What the he-"

They cover my mouth and hold my hand tight. I see men running around the store. I look to my side to see who has held my mouth and arms so tight, but unfortunately because of the darkness, I can't see their face. The men finally leave and they pull me out of the corner. Before I could even thank them, they leave.

I start to shiver vigourously. I might need bodyguards now. Who was that person though? Why was the tattoo on their hand and finger so familiar? It was almost as if I've seen it somewhere but I've not.

ꕥ

I get to the parking lot and reach my rolls royce phantom black matte. My assistant helps me with my shopping bags and the driver opens the door for me. I get inside and sit in the back. I turn my phone on and all I can see are notifications from the news site. It's about the jewellery store incident. I zoom in to see if I can find the person but no site of them. The tattoo is getting to me. It was an eagle tattoo on his hand and a heart on his index finger. It was like deja vu.

I finally reach my mansion and the cleaners help me carry away my shopping bags. I reach my room and freshen up. I'm wearing a robe with a glass of wine in my hand. Today was hectic. I NEED this glass of wine. I look outside the view from my bedroom window and it's the most beautiful sight I've witnessed. I remember father specially fighting with the owners to get this room only for me. I'm admirring the view and this wine goes perfect with it. I hear a knock on my door. I turn back, place the wine glass on my table and walk towards the door. I ask who it is but there's no answer. I ask again but this time, the door barges open. I lean against the wall behind the door as my heart starts pounding outside of my chest.

"What the actual he-"

I almost say but someone from behind me covers my mouth and drags me to my chair. I'm scared now. Who are these people? After he places me on my chair, he lets go of me. The guy infront of me gestures him to move. He's wearing a mask, with an all black outfit. After a few seconds, I realize I'm all tied up. Someone then barges in. They run towards the guy infront of me and gestures him to leave. They come closer to my eyes, have a stare then lean back. He takes his mask off and there he was. Head of the French unit, Romain Vanchover. He's someone I've never wanted to see but there he was, standing in front of me after 2 years. He gives me this evil smile. God, I hate that smile.

It hasn't changed. Tears are dripping down my face. I wasn't expecting this. I wasn't expecting him to come fter 2 years. I'm finally set free from the damn tissue papers in my mouth with my hands still tied behind my back.

"WHAT DO YOU WANT?" I scream.

He chuckles.

"I want you." He says.

I start to look at him with death in my eyes.

"2 years ago, I had held your father so tight, but you barged in... Such a party pooper." He sys as he's roaming around the bedroom, touching through everything.

"My son could've told you about this plan, but he didn't."

He's talking about Navon.

"WHY DIDN'T HE?" I screamed again.

"Because, he wanted you."

That doesn't make sense at all.

"I made it clear, I don't want him or his family."

He chuckles. I'm really confused. He starts to walk more towards me, tries to whisper something but I can't hear because I then push him with my feet and break open the rope that had tied me. He places his hand on his stomach and falls to the ground on his back. He groans in pain.

I quicky open my drawer and take my gun out and point it towards him. He has his hands in the air as he stands up. He backs up as I get closer. He starts to laugh.

"I'm leaving this time, but mark my words, you will regret it."

And he leaves.

I fall to the ground and start to breakdown like it's the end of the world. Why is the French unit still after me? I was done with them.

V

Chapter five

"They're after the company."

That can't be! It's my company. Dad passed it on me. It was already written on his will.

"That can't be!" I say banging my fists on the table.

The assistant of the Italian force calms me down. The Italian force had reached out to me after the jewellery store incident. I had to make sure it was them for real.

"Your father never made a statement at his party that the company would be passed on to you, knowing this, they're after you and your company, despite it being written on his will."

Stress in me builds up more and more. True that father never announced it but it's there, written on his will. I've submitted the documents as well, regarding I being the next CEO.

After a few minutes, we're done with the meeting and we've come to a conclusion that I'm in need of bodyguards. We bid our goodbyes to each other and my assistant calls out for me.

"There's someone for you at the entrance."

I nod as a sign to let them in. My glass windows on the side of my door clearly shows the hand of the person standing behind the door. I try to focus my eyes and see the same eagle and heart tattoo. The door opens and I finally see him, except it's not a 'he'. It's a 'she'. It was a woman who saved me?

"Ms. Daphne, isn't it?" oh God, the way I want the 'ms' to change into 'captain'.

She looks masculine. No wonder I thought it's a 'he'. I nod and offer her a seat. She takes a seat and looks serious.

"How may I help you?" I ask.

She rests her elbow on the table facing forward towards me. She takes a breath and finally speaks.

"I'm Silvia Valence, I was the one who held you during the incident in the jewellery store. I came here to speak to you about something important."

I'm more serious now. I wait for her to continue speaking.

"It's about... Navon, and the whole French unit."

Some kind of anger builds up in me, wanting to strangle Navon to death. Something about him gets me so worked up.

I sigh and close my eyes.

"It's going to be hard for you to listen, but do listen."

I sigh and cover my face with my hands.

"Yes, I'm sorry, please tell me." I say.

Silvia kind off hesitates but eventually, "Your father has sent me here to you. He's alive and held hostage."

My eyes widen, my jaw drops. This can't be! It's been 2 years. I start to ugly cry while Silvia tries to calm me down. I can't believe it. I don't know how to believe it. Father is alive! I need to see him. I have to, I want to!

"I never came to tell you this because, I too am from the French unit. But your father and I have been really close. Right now, I'm under no unit, I'm just an ordinary person trying to help your father. He's like a father to me as well."

Silvia says.

I don't know how to react anymore so I just cry on Silvia's shoulders. I cry so much, I feel so weak. Silvia has to hold me tight. A few minutes pass by and Silvia starts explaining about everything that happened that night.

"You passed out due to shock and tension while having your father in your arms. I was there too but no one knew because I had sneaked in. I understand this might be a lot for you. But this is a matter of your father. While you passed out, Navon and his father took your father away. After they left, I took you to the hospital and left."

Navon? Navon took my father away? I thought he was trying to stop his father.

"Navon? I thought he was trying to stop his father. How could he have?" I ask.

Silvia looks at me like she's hiding something. she looks down at her tattoo and caresses it with her fingers. I raise an eyebrow at her.

"Um Silvia?"

"The thing is... Navon is my brother, his father is also my father, but I had cut ties with them long ago, all because of Navon and his father. Something happened. Something very bad."

Oh good Lord, this is a lot in one day. This is another shocker.

"If you don't mind me asking, what happened?" I ask looking at her as she looks down at her tattoo.

She sighs.

"That's something I can't say. For now let's concentrate on saving your father."

I smile and nod.

"Silvia, can I ask you something?" she nods as a yes.

"Have we met somewhere other than the jewellery store? That tattoo is really familiar."

Silvia smiles and looks at her tattoo.

"Please call me Silvi. But yeah you might've seen this tattoo on my brother. We have matching ones. So you know, Navon is not a bad guy. It's just our father spoiling him. So, if you could marry the desparate guy-"

We laugh.

"No really, he's a good guy. I miss him dearly." Silvia says.

I honestly can not trust anyone right now. Navon makes me want to punch the wall so hard that the building collapses. Just then, I get a call from the landline. I pick it up and I can hear static. That's all I hear. I tell Silvia about this. She panics as if something has happened.

VI

Chapter six

We're in the car, Silvia is rushing through the streets. The statics was giving us an address. It was father trying to communicate with us. Trying to call out for help. We're on the way there. After a few minutes, we reach this very isolated forest. We walk through it and see a cabin. A small hut like cabin. We bang the door and hear no response. We kick the door and it breaks open. I see father all tied up, injured and cold. I run to him crying, immidiately untie him and hug him tight. I cry on his shoulders. He can barely talk, he's gotten so weak.

Silvia is standing beside us and smiling. Just then we hear footsteps. I look behind while still having father in my arms. Silvia looks worried.

"QUICK! TAKE HIM TO THE CAR! IT'S FATHER AND NAVON!"

I quickly take father with me. His arms are around my shoulders and I walk him towards the car. He's light as a feather now, I've missed him so much.

Just as I'm placing father in the car I hear Silvia scream.

I give father some water and food that I got on the way and ask him to stay in the car while I get Silvia. I run towards the cabin and see Navon standing there by the side watching his father beat Silvia up. I run towards Silvia and pull her aside. Navon tries to stop his father. I immidiately take Silvia alone with meand place her in the car. I take the drivers seat and start to drive. I hear gun shots in the background.

VII

Chapter seven

Seeing Navon after 2 years made me feel some type of way. I felt some type of connection. It never felt as though he was an enemy of mine. Maybe my mind always wanted to strangle him to death but my heart always wanted to choke him with love. I don't know I feel this way.

Father wakes up and I call for the doctors. The doctors come in and check his well being.

"He's fine, he's just weak and can only be okay once he starts having regular meals."

The doctor leaves and I give father a peck on his forehead. He goes back to sleep and I hear a knock on the door. The door opens and I see Silvia.

"Silvi, how're you doing?"

"I'm doing great now actually. I've something to talk to you about." I smile and nod. I gesture her to talk in the garden outside.

We're walking back and forth as Silvia starts talking.

"About the French head, you don't have to worry about that anymore. Navon killed him."

A sigh of relief releases from me.

"And about Navon, he's no longer under the French unit."

I raise my eyebrow.

"What? Why?" I ask.

"He did that for you."

As I hear that, My stomach is in tangles now when it shouldn't be. He's an enemy. It should be this way.

"Look, the reason I cut ties wih father and Navon is because when Navon and I were 12 and 14, our parents got into a huge fight. Navon being the older brother, I expected him to take care of me, but he didn't. Our father had made this plan to go after our mother and he'd involded Navon in it. Later, mother passed away because father held the gun with Navons hand and shoot her. Navon had no idea whatsoever of what was going on. I was mad at my family and I had never seen them ever since mother passed away until the day before yesterday. Our father was not a good man. Killing got him pleasure. I left home and was put into an adoption center. I went from foster home to foster home until I realized I can't do this anymore, so I started my own modeling career and fashion company. Until I met thi really sweet family who had been willing to take me. And now, I'm their daughter. That's why I'm Silvia Valence and he is Navon Vanchover. I'm happy now."

I smile at her. She's a very strong independent woman. I like how she's built herself even after going through so much. I express this to her. Then I ask, "what about Navon and you now?"

She smiles.

"We're good. I met him this morning. He's waiting for you."

Silvia says and my smile drops so fast. There's no expression on my face. I simply can not. What was he doing when his father bet Silvia up? What was he doing when my father was all tied up? I can't trust him so fast so easily. This is my time to be with father. His health is way more important than Navon. Silvia looks like she's waiting for a responseout of me.

"Listen Daph, I know what you're thinking, before you say anything-"

"Silvi, I can't. Right now, Father is my priority. I don't think I can trust him just yet. I hope you understand."

Silvia smiles and spreads her arms out for a hug. I give her a hug giving her a smile back.

"I understand." Silvia says as she pulls back.

"I have to go to father now."

Silvia nods.

VIII

Chapter eight

Father is finally home and healthy. He just needs to take his medications on time. I‘m really happy that father is home now. I'm going to make up for lost time. It's been a month since I've seen Silvia. We had a few texts here and there but nothing more than that. I had a random thought about her today. I wonder how she's doing. Father calls out to me in the living room. I got to him and he spreads his arms and gives me a warm smile. I run towards him and hug him while I lay on his chest. It feels so good to be in fathers arms again.

"I‘m proud of you Daph." Father says while he pats my head. I smile.

"You should also be proud of yourself father. You survived."

I say looking up at him.

"I survived because of you. You saved me on time."

I start to tear up but I manage hiding it.

"I love you father."

"I love you more Daph."

Father pinches my nose. There's this sweet silence.

I somehow break it and ask, "Father, what about the company?"

Father smiles, he gets up and sits back up properly making us sit side by side.

"What about it Daph?"

"Do you want to head CEO, or chase your plane?"

I SQUEL! Father accepts it. Oh God, I feel so joyful right now. I cover my mouth with my hands and ask,

"Can I? Can I really chase that plane father?"

Father smiles and nods. I scream in joy and happiness. I jump into fathers arms and hug him so tight. Oh God, I hope nothing goes wrong! I know everything will go right. I won't let father regret this.

"I promise I'm going to make me so successful."

Father chuckles as I say that.

"What are you waiting for? Go ahead! Start searching for airline academies."

I get up from the sofa and turn back in question.

"Father, the company?"

"Selling it to our beloved Itaian unit."

I feel so happy. This moment feels so surreal. We're not in the Spain unit anymore.

"Father, YOU WON'T REGRET THIS!" I scream in joy and head to my room.

I immidiately turn my laptop on and start searching for airline academies. Since I've already written the examinations for this, I could dirctly go for admissions. But for this, I'm gonna need a lot of thinking. There is this academy that is all the way across the world that I'm willing to go to. But right now, I have to stay by my father's side. I can't leave him right now. He needs all my support.

I'm browsing through academies until I see California's academy of Air. The academy all the way across the world that I want to go to. I hesitate to click on it even though it's always been a dream of mine. Right now all I have on mind is I'm going to become a pilot! How exciting is that I'm clogged with joy and happiness. All this is possible because of Father. I'm so grateful to him. You know what I just want to cry on his shoulders saying thank you.

I close my laptop shut and open my door with tears already forming in my eyes. I search for him, calling out to him and no sign of him. I go to his room and see him lying on the floor unconscious. My smile drops.

I rush towards him and lace his head on my lap as I slap his face while I call out to him.

"Father? Father! Let's get you to bed. Don't sleep here! Father?!"

I slap him multiple times yet no response from him. I start to tear up but force a smile at the same time. He's not responding so I check his pulse, and put my finger under his nose. He's not breathing. This is a joke right? He's playing a prank on me.

"Father! Wake up! I know it's a joke, see I'm laughing, Ha Ha Ha."

I keep forcing a laugh until realization hits that he's gone. I stop laughing and hug him so tight. I start to cry with hiccups as I'm hugging him. I cry out loud like the world has ended. But for me, my world has ended. My father, my only hero. I can't believe I lost him. I don't want to believe I lost him.

ꕥ

The ambulance arrives and they take father away. I'm all alone at home, sitting in father's room. I see his laptop open.

I go through it. I see a folder named 'hi Daph'.

I look in confusion and click on the folder. I see a 3 minute long video.

I place myself on his bed and the laptop on the bed table. I'm not prepared for what's about to come. I click play anyways.

It's father trying to set the camera and sits up right and says,

Hey Daph! My princess. I can't promise this video will reach to you but if it does then listen. You might me watching this moments after I've gone to heaven. Don't cry, I'm safe up here. Daph, you know I've gotten old and weak. Especially since the past two years, I had not been able to have a proper meal. This media is after me. So are many other units. I can't be dealing with all this at this age. So I want to say, it's for the best that I left. At least I'm safe up here, in heaven. I'm living my time, except I'm not living haha. Daph, just know that I love you so much. I always have. I want you to live your life before you come join me. So, go ahead! Apply for the academy. It would make me so amazing-ly happy to see you fly up high, close to me. Even if I'm not there, remember, I'm always in your heart. I love you so much Daph.

Oh God, I'm crying again. This time, he's gone. For good. I don't want to believe it, but I'm going to have to. I'm hugging his pillow as I bawl my eyes out.

Father, I love you so much, I'm going to make you so proud.

IX

Chapter nine

"For everyone who has come here today, on this day where we bid our goodbyes to my father, thank you so much for coming."

I start to tear up. I never thought I'd have to say goodbye so early. I see everyone here just mourning over father but they never cared about him. I'm looking down at the grave where father is buried, and I place some flowers on it. I stare at it for a few minutes.I don't want to believe this. I really hope that at some point, father could tap on my shoulder and tell me that this was all a huge prank. I wouldn't even have gotten back. I just want my father back. Tears started rolling down my cheek. Just then I feel a tap on my shoulder. I turn around to see Silvia. I look at her and start crying more and more as she pulls me into a hug where I could cry on her shoulders. She pats my head and asks me to calm down. After a few seconds, I pull back.

"You're so strong Daphne, you got this. He is looking at you right now, he wouldn't want to see you this way."

Silvia says and hands me a napkin to wipe my tears off. I take it from her hand and wipe them off. Silvia smiles and places a sunflower on his grave.

"It was his favourite ones, wasn't it?" I smile and nod.

Indeed, sunflowers were his favourite.

"Daph, may I ask you something?"

Silvia asks with doe eyes that turned from siren eyes.

"How did it happen?" I was hoping she wouldn't ask this.

I take a huge deep breath and answer,

"Suicide. He did not want any more problems. He thought it'd be better off in heaven."

Silvia sighs and shuts her eyes.

"Daph, you father, was a wise man." I smile in terms that I agree.

Silvia takes a huge sigh and says, "There's something I haven't told you. About your father that I think you should know."

I raise my eyebrows in question as I look at her. My heart rate increases. I'm curious to know what's up now. Silvia holds my hand and takes a breath.

"Your father had saved my life." I smile. Tears are forming again. I knew father was an amazing man. I let Silvia continue.

FLASHBACK IN SILVIA'S POV

Just like I thought, another foster home. Will this ever end? Will I ever be able to find a decent family? or is it just my fate. I give up now. I'm only 17 years old. I should be going to the mall with my friends, travelling around the world, but no, this is my destiny. Honestly, I am done with this life of mine. I just want a family who's ready to adopt me for me and not foster me for the money. Is that so hard for a wish at the age of 17? I'm on the bed when I hear the front door opening. It's probably my foster parents leaving the house. I get back on my phone and scroll through it for a good 15 minutes, until I smell something burning.

I can smell gasoline, fire and wood outside my room. I try stepping out by opening the door but I see smoke entering into my room. I fall to the ground, covering my mouth and coughing. I eventually get up, and open the door only to see fire. I try to get out of there, but the entire hallway is just fire. Would my foster parents want to do this to me? I close the door of my bedroom and try opening the window, but it's locked!

I forgot my foster parents have the key. I start the banging the window in hope that someone comes for me. At this point I'm losing consciousness, but just then the window breaks into millions of pieces of shattered glass. It's like someone threw a rock. Someones hand enters through the window, signaling me to hold on. I hold on and they pull me out. The whole house is on fire, that moment someone was just in time to save me. I can barely keep my eyes open, because of the heat and my body had gone so weak from trying to break the window. I fall conscious into that someones arms.

The next time I wake up, I woke up in the hospital.

"Where am I?"

The doctor looks at me, and says, "You're on the hospital bed, your house was on fire and we almost lost you because of the smoke which had reached your lungs. Thank God someone was just in time to save you."

I want to know who that someone is. That someone also saved my life before I almost lost it. My body feels so numb and all I can see is needles around me. I can only open my eyes and hear through my ears. I can barely speak or move my body. The only thing working right now are my thoughts and sounds of the monitors were so audible. Just then, a man in a black suit walks in towards me. I have an oxygen mask on me so I can't say anything.

He sits beside me on my hospital bed and caresses my head. He smiles and says, "one day, make me proud, that's the biggest thank you I could get."

I give a slight smile with all my capability in response to him. I smile knowing he's the one who had saved me. I start to tear up and soon after tears start rolling down my cheeks. He frowns and wipes my tears away. He then says,

"Marcom White, find me whenever you can."

He gets up and leaves. I try to catch his arm, but I've gotten so weak. Marcom White, I will find you, give you the biggest thank you I can.

END OF FLASHBACK

BACK TO DAPHNES POV

Oh God, listening to all this, makes me so proud of father. He's done so much for the world. I'm really proud to be the daughter of Marcom White.

We end up sitting on the bench nearby.

"I have no words, Silvia. Is that how you found father?"

Silvia smiles as I ask. She holds my hand and scoochs closer to me, and says,

"Your father is too great for no one to be able to have recognized him. I saw on the news and found it suspicious. So, I went on a search for him. The reason I launched my own company is because of him. He's the reason. I wanted to show him how thankful I am. I hope he's seen it."

I smile and hold Silvia's hand tighter. She looks at me with a proud face on.

"I'm sure, he wants the same for you."

Just wait and watch father, as I make you the proudest father on plant.

ꝏ

X

Chapter ten

I bite my nails in fear. What if I get rejected? My heart is beating out of my chest now. I'm sweating vigorously. This is the moment. The moment I've been waiting for my entire life. I can not mess this up! Not now, I can't! The application says ready and I click on 'open'. Just when I'm opening it, I'm shaking so much and my heart rate feels higher than the length from ground to sky. It takes a few seconds to load.

CONGRATULATIONS!! We are delighted to inform you that you've been accepted to ***California's academy of air.***

I squel. Yes oh my God! I did it! I almost tear up but Silvia shakes me out of it,

"You're going to be amazing, Captain."

Silvia gives me a tight hug. Oh my God, I still can't believe it! Just a few years and I'll become captain! Father would've been really proud of me. I'm sure he's watching down on me and he's really proud of me. He's yapping to his mates in heaven about me haha.

Silvia gets a call and excuses herself. She takes her phone out, and goes to the corner. She picks up the phone and screams, "CONGRATULATIONS BRO I'M SO PROUD OF YOU!"

I'm too busy admiring the application of mine. I'm going to have this framed. That's for sure. Silvia heads back.

"Dude, what're you waiting for? GO! start packing."

I jump towards my room. This time, I take silvia with me.

ꝏ

We somehow end up in a nearby cafe. We're sipping on coffee. Except I'm not sipping on coffee, I'm sipping on tea. I'm a tea person more than a coffee person.

Silvia takes a sip of her coffee and looks at me while she keeps the cup on the table.

"So, -pause- how do you feel?"

Oh God, how do I feel? I feel out of this world. I can't describe the way I feel right now.

"I feel... like a proud daughter. I feel like I've given father the biggest thank you I've ever given."

Silvia smiles at my response. I take a sip of my tea and look outside the window. As I do so, I see a familiar hand, with an eagle tattoo. I look back at Silvia's hand all confused.

"Silvi, does anyone else have the same tattoo as you do?" Silvia looks down at her tattoo and says,

"Yeah, Navon and I got it together when we were kids. I mean, our father had forced us to, why?"

Just then the front entrance of the cafe turns open. Both Silvia and I look towards thedoor only to see Navon standing there. Oh God, what's he doing here? Why's he here? He's walking towards us.

I give Silvia, 'the eyes' like did you call him on purpose. But oh Lord doesn't he look magnificent? His hazelnut eyes, his 6'0 self and black curly wavy hair. His body is so bulked up and muscular. Oh boy, Daph, snap out of it! He didn't do shit when father was held hostage, remember? You hate him remember? Oh but do I?

I hide my face as he's approaching us.

"Hey sis, celebrating without me? The main person?" -looks at daphne- I didn't know you had company. Hi! I'm Navon, and you are?"

Well shit, now I have to turn my face around. I slowly turn my face into his direction until I'm under his gaze.

"Hello again Navon." I could he's shocked to see me.

"Okay guys, this wasn't on purpose I swear. I just-"

Silvia says but Navon cuts her off,

"Why are you here?"

Huh? What the actual hell, this is my day, what does he mean?

"Umm, why are you here? It's my day." I say with the same attitude back.

"So is for me. This is a brother-sister time. You can LEAVE!"

"NAVON! SHUT UP!" Silvia screams and we have everyones attention. Navon flinches as she does so. Silvia gestures him to shit down. He sits down obediently.

"Both of you got into the same university. DEAL WITH IT! I'm so tired of hiding shit from the both of you."

My eyes widen as Silvia says so. ME? NAVON? SAME UNIVERSITY? NO! NO! NO!

I point towards him in a questionable way and say,

"Why bro?"

He raises his eyebrow.

"The hell do you mean by bro? Also, it's a dream of mine. To start an airline after becoming a captain."

He wasn't lying when he said he was just like me.

"Deal with each other now and stop this shit before I bury the both of you alive." Silvia says.

XI

Chapter eleven

"I'm sorry ma'am. Your flight has been delayed until tomorrow morning."

WHAT! Flight delayed? Where will I go? I'm packed out. Silvia is pushing me to be with Navon too now. Another headache with me.

"We don't have anywhere else to go, what do you mean?" Navon says to the person in charge.

"We'll book a hotel for the both of you. Have a seat until then."

Navon bangs his stuff and takes a seat. I follow behind him and take a seat two chairs away from him.

"It's because of you!" I scream.

"Me? I'm not the pilot bruh."

We argue and after a few hours reach the hotel.

ꙮ

"Welcome! How may I help you?"

The receptionist says.

"Two rooms please." Navon says.

The receptionist nods and shifts her eyes towards the monitor infront of her. Her expression doesn't look too good. May the Lord allow rooms to be available, Amen.

"I'm sorry sir. Unfortunately we only hhave 1 room available with a king sized bed."

I'd rather sleep on the streets than share a bed with Navon. I can hear Navon sighing and rolling his eyes.

"Are you sure it's correct? What if there's a glitch on the system?"

I ask in stress.

"We'll take it." Navon says immidiately.

The receptionist smiles, so that's it. He's okay with it.

"Your good name sir."

For some reason Navon hesitates to answer.

"Navon Zayne Vanchover."

Zayne? Since when did he have Zayne in his name.

"Zayne?" I ask.

"Yeah..." He responds with a long stretch. He looks away. He seems embarrased of his name. After an hour, we settle down in the room.

"This side is mine. DO NOT CROSS THIS!" I say as I place pillows between the bed. I look up only to see Navon standing there with his arms folded. He's wearing a black hoodie with rolled up sleeves where his veins are more than just visible. His thick eyebrows when he's serious and his messy black hair looks so hot.

I can't be falling for him, but somewhere inside I want him. I can't be seen blushing around him.

"Are you going to help?" I ask getting back into my senses.

He smiles. That smile is very manipulative, very... save me.

"Sit down for sometime. I want to talk." He says. He sits down on the chair, just manspreading. He pulls out a chair for me and signals me to sit down. I take a seat.

"Listen, Daphne, I want to clear up whatever is going on. I feel like there is a clear misunderstanding."

A misunderstanding is the last thing I thought about.

"I'm listening."

I say with a very serious look on my face.

Navon takes a deep breath in, and he says,

"When I said I'd leave everyone and everything for you, I wasn't kidding. I killed my father in worry that he'd be after you again and again. I've never liked my father. I hated him in every possible way. I also feared him so I couldn't save my own sister. I have a dream of becoming a pilot, start an airline. That day, I tried my best to stop father, but he wasn't budging. The reason why I revealed to you about passing the company to you is because I wanted you to save you father. I also didn't know about your father being held hostage. It was only that day when you came that I found out. Daph, I've been waiting for you, since the past two years, and I will still wait for you whenever you're ready."

I have no words literally. I don't know what to say. Maybe he is saying the truth. But I can't trust him right now. It's too soon.

"Navon, I need time."

Navon smiles and nods. I don't know what to do so I get up and lie down on the bed until I sleep.

Not now Navon, show me you love me, and so I will.

XII

Chapter twelve

NAVON POV

I hate Silvia for making us go together. Daphne clearly still hates me. What am I supposed to do to prove that I love her. I love her to the universe and on. She's facing me as we're sleeping. Well, she's sleeping. She looks really cute. I remove the pillow that's kept as a barrier between us. I can see her much better now. She looks like a kitten when she's asleep. It's so cute. She unconsciously puts her arm around me. Oh God, what do I? Would she be comfortable? I mean, she's unconscious. She's sleeping. I smile at her cuteness and forget about these questions. I pull her closer to me by her waist.

She murmurs in her sleep,

"Navon, I want you too."

She speaks in her sleep. The way I wish that this line is true is insane. AND SHE SMILES!

"I want you more." I whisper. I give her a soft peck on her forehead and I fall asleep.

THE NEXT MORNING

We're waiting for boarding and I see Daphne sitting in front of me on her phone. I go sit beside her and she looks at me with fed up eyes.

"You don't remember last night, do you?" I ask. Daphne raises her eyebrows and looks at me,

"What?" She asks. She doesn't and how could she.

"I mean... Nothing." I want her to cling on to me and ask me what happened.

And like I thought, she did.

"Don't play with me and tell me for God's sake." She says.

SHE DEMANDS.

I chuckle before I say anything then I say everything. She turns red. She looks embarrased. It's so cute.

"Aww, you want me?" I say very playfully. She hits me. I forgot how hard mafia women hit.

OUCH! Daphne White, I know you want me too but not as much as I want you.

XIII

Chapter thirteen

BACK TO DAPHNE'S POV

"Isn't that... Daphne white?" Says one.

"OH MY GOD! DAPHNE WHITE? WHAT'S SHE DOING WITH NAVON VANCHOVER?" Says another.

People murmur as we're going down the stairs to the dias to introduce themselves. I forgot I was famous.

I FORGOT I AM FAMOUS.

I have been famous for the wrong reason, ugh. Navon is looking at me as he has his arms out in signal that he wants me to hold on to his forearm.

"You said you want me, so why hesitate to hold me?"

I regret saying each and every word I said that night. I don't even remember what I said, and why I said it.

"I know you hate huge steps, I know you're scared of them. I could tell when you walked in."

He suddenly stops and waits for me to hold him.

"I don't get why you're so afraid, you're going to fly high."

The cameras of the students flashes and screams for us are so loud. I can barely hear him but I can. The professor asks them to settle down. I take his hand in embarrasment and walk to the dias. We introduce ourselves which there was no need of because everyone already clearly knows us and who we are.

We take a seat near the last few places. As I sit down, I hear a male voice greeting me.

"Hi Daphne."

I turn around and I say hello back.

"I'm Rider. Nice to meet you."

Rider says. He seems like a nice guy. He reaches his hand out for a handshake. I shake his hands.

"Is that your boyfriend?"

He points to Navon asking this. Navon looks back and looks at Rider.

"No no. He's my-"

"Boyfriend! Yes, boyfriend."

I look at Navon. I'm not mad for some reason. Right now, my stomach is in knots and tangles. What do I feel? I don't know what to feel. A huge part of me has butterflies who wanted him to say that.

"Oh that's nice! I hope we can be good friends."

Rider says.

"Of course we can. Nice to meet you Rider. I'm Navon."

What's Navon trying to do? I can't tell if he's trying to take control over who I am friends with or if he's trying to protect me. Navon turns back and I ask,

"What was that for?"

I ask him making eye contact with him.

"You never know how men are like."

Navon says and he turns to face the dias while I still look at him in confusion.

ꕥ

"Look at the board, not me."

I blush and face forward. Why am I blushing? I'm not supposed to be blushing dude what the hell.

Navon, you make me go crazy.

ꙮ

After a few hours, we're done with the introduction for today and we're headed back to the apartments.

Rider runs behind us.

"Hey guys, could you guys give me a ride to my apartment?"

Navon nods. We direct Rider to our car and he sits in the front seat while Navon is driving. We're all seated and on the way.

"So, Rider, tell me about yourself. Why airline?"

Rider smiles and gulps as Navon asks. I'm sitting in the backseat just watching them talk. I can't even say anything because I don't know what to say.

"Let's talk about something else, how long have you guys been together?"

Well, that was weird. I did not expect Rider to just change the subject. And what kind of a trap has Navon gotten us in to. Like what should I answer to that question?

"2 weeks."

Navon replies.

"Oh wow, it's been 2 weeks with my girlfriend too."

Rider says. I wonder who the lucky girl is. So I ask,

"Who's she? Spill!"

I ask leaning forward, curious to know. I mean who wuldn't fall for Rider, Look at him. This blue eyed wavy long hair. Oh God. I'm not falling for him though. I can't, and I don't know why. Something tells me that I need to be loyal to Navon but we're not even together.

"She's not into airline, she's in Valence academy of Fashion."

VALENCE? SILVIA VALENCE? Navon gasps causing Rider to flinch.

"Are you okay??"

Rider asks but Navon is still in shock. Silvia has academies as well? I thought she's just a CEO of a Fashion company.

"That's my sister's academy. I mean she owns it! Like the multiple branches."

Navon exclaims like the proud brother he is.

"DAMN! Small world eh? Silvia Valence is YOUR sister, I didn't know."

Navon smiles as he hears Silvias name coming out of Riders mouth.

"What is your girlfriends name?" I ask. He blushes at the thought of his girlfriend. That's so cute. I want a guy who would blush at the thought of his girlfriend.

"She's Raegan."

Rider says and smiles. Raegan rings a bell for some reason. I had a childhood friend whom I lost touch with like 2 years ago. Maybe it's a different Raegan.

We reach Riders destination. He gets off, but before he leaves he says..

"Thank you Navon Vanchover."

"Thank you Rider-"

Navon pauses.

"Rider Flynn."

"It's like the movie! I like the name."

Navon smiles.

"Go now, take care, see you tomorrow."

I smile at him, roll down my window and say,

"You and Raegan seem real cute, make sure to take care of your rapunzel well."

Rider smiles.

XIV

Chapter fourteen

It's been a month since pilot training has started. It's been going well. Two days ago, Navon and I decided we are not going to try to kill each other everyday and commit murder because we have to stay together for a really long time. He's still my fake boyfriend, which I'm still pretty mad about. But honestly, I kind of want that fake to be real. I've been noticing some changes whatever Navon does gives me the worst butterflies. I can't handle it sometimes. Navon has been flirting with me too like A LOT! He's been giving me many hints.

It's morning right now, I'm in my tank top and shorts. My hair is in a messy bun. I'm making my morning tea and Navons stupid morning coffee, because that idiot doesn't know how to make coffee. Just as I'm making it, I feel a hand caressesing my waist. I turn around only to see Navon.

"Good morning Monkey face."

He says and removes the hair tie that was holding my bun on to for dear life.

"NAVON!" I scream.

He's so childish sometimes ugh!

"I'm not making your COFFEE!" I scream. I can see he doesn't give a shit. I don't give a shit either. He can make it himself.

I go to him with an angry face.

"When are you leaving my flat?"

I fold my arms and look at him. He puts my hair tie on his hand and just looks at me.

"God damn you look so hot right now."

Navon says.

NO! NO! NO! He can't do this to me. I crack a smile and look away.

"Go! Leave!"

I say.

Navon is just there laughing and smiling at me and just admiring me like I'm this craving he wants. Not in that way. My guy's obsessed with food.

"Alright! I'm leaving! But please be mad at me more often, it's so hot."

He says and he leaves. What if I go to him right now and tell him I like him and I seriously want him? Would anything happen? Would Daphne and Navon happen? I so badly want to. But I'm scared. Mostly of rejection.

It's the afternoon on a sunday and I'm in my car waiting for Navon. He's taking too long and it's starting to get annoying. He finally comes out blushing. Why the hell is he blushing? I lock the door as he tries to open it. I roll the window down,

"Why're you blushing?"

I ask with a stern face.

"What do you mean?"

Navon asks.

"You're blushing, who is it?" Why am I getting so defensive of him, I'm not even dating him.

"Dude, open the door. It's hot outside."

Navon exclaims.

"Tell me, and I will."

I say looking serious.

"What if I don't?"

Navon asks. I say okay in the dry-est way possible and roll up my window and start to drive. He's chasing the car as I'm driving. I'm feeling generous so I stop the car. He's panting heavily and I roll down the window.

"I swear I'll tell you, just let me in."

I look at him and unlock the door. He comes inside and immidiately turns all the ACs to himself. I stare at him waiting for him to tell me.

"Drive, I'll tell you."

I start to drive and he takes a breath.

"It's someone from training. She's been really nice to me."

Navon says.

Oh...

Well, not like I'm jealous right? Okay maybe I am but I'm not going to show it.

"You're jealous aren't you?"

Hell bruh! It's too visible.

"Me? Jealous? No, it's her loss!"

Navon chuckles as I say that.

"She's just a friend. I don't like her so don't worry princess."

HE JUST CALLED ME WHAT? My stomach, I can't! Oh how I wish I could take you as my prince.

XV

Chapter fifteen

"I hope you guys can come? It's like THE EVENT OF THE YEAR."

One of our classmates says. I smile and nod and say that I'll try to. I focus on my food now. The cafeteria lunch is not as bad as I thought. Navon is infront of me just stuffing his face with food. Just then a girl walks by him while caressesing his shoulders from left to right. Navon and her make eye contact and give each other a flirty smile. It's killing me for some reason. I can't help but show it through my expressions.

"What happened?"

Navon asks.

"Nothing. I'll see you at the party."

I say as I get up and head towards the exit. I feel like crying. Why is it affecting me so much? I need father right now. But I know I can't. He's gone and there's nothing I can do about it. I run towards the car and sit on the drivers seat and just bawl my eyes out. I cry so much that my eyes have gone puffy. I love him. I wanted him to wait for me. I want him so bad. It's like both my worlds have ended.

I take my phone out and text my trainer.

me: Hey, I'll not be coming today, as I've fallen sick. Hope you'll excuse me this time.

trainer: Oh take care. Do come up on sunday so I can teach you whatever you missed.

me: Thank you :)

I switch my phone off and head home. Tears are still rolling down my face. After a few minutes, I reach home. I go straight to my room and cry a little more on my pillow. I shouldn't be crying so much for a guy. But I love him.

BACK AT THE ACADEMY, NAVON POV

I walked in to the training center with Rider. I'm still thinking about Daphne. Why's she acting so weird lately? Speaking of Daphne, I look around to see where she is. She's nowhere to be found. I ask Rider where she is while still looking at her.

"You don't know? She fell sick. She took a leave."

Rider says. I instantly face him. She was fine till lunch, what happened? Something is going on. I can't leave her like this.

"Rider, tell the trainer that I'm sick too. I have to go after her."

Rider nods, and I go running. I start the car and rush to the apartments. I really hope it's nothing. What did I say, that's making her act so weird? If it's about Gracia, I don't give a shit about Gracia. I see her as a friend. That actually might be it. Oh God, I love you Daphne, why can't you see that?

I reach her flat door and ring the bell multiple times. But there's no response. I bang on the door asking her to open. I know she's in there right on the sofa.

"Listen Daphne, I know you're not sick. You're completely fine. If you open the door, we can just talk about it."

Again, there's no response.

"Daph, please!" No response again. I know she's in there probably crying and bawling her eyes out on the sofa while she hugs a pillow. Maybe she needs time.

"You know what Daph, I'm going to sit outside until you open the door."

I casually sit on the ground. I don't care if it's 3 AM as well, I'm waiting there until she comes out.

BACK TO DAPHNES POV

I'm holding on to a pillow and bawling my eyes out as I am sitting on the sofa. I don't respond to Navon. I need my time

ꕥ

I'm wearing this black bodycon mini dress with upto knee heels and I have my hair open.

As I open the door, I see Navon sleeping outside the door. I can't look at him right now, I need to clear my mind. So, I'm off to the party. After half an hour, I reach and see Rider there. I rush to him and say hi.

"You look gorgeous."

Rider says.

"Thank you, you look gorgeous yourself."

I reply.

Rider signals me as to where Navon is. I shake my head and I say that I don't know. Rider then points behind me and I turn back only to see Navon. Navon looks at me and smiles but I ignore him and rush to the restroom.

Rider tries to stop me, but it's too late. I try stopping myself from crying and I see Gracia coming out of the restroom. Just great. I pretend as though I'm doing my makeup because she CANNOT see me crying.

"You know Daphne, Navon is an amazing guy."

She says as she's washing her hands. She's done and she looks at me and says.

"I feel that's changing considering he's cheating on me."

She gives this evil smile and walks towards the door. She stops again and says,

"Just a girl-to-girl advice, he's not for you."

She says and leaves. I'm not angry. I'm furious. I literally can't. I rush outside only to see Gracia clinging on to Navon. Navon notices that I've seen it. I run outside the house as Navon follows me.

"Daph! Wait!" He screams.

I'm outside the house crying so much. It starts to rain. Navon follows me outside and grabs my hand.

"Daphne, please. Let's just talk about this."

Navon says with tears in his eyes. I look at him but do not listen. I try going back but he's held on to me so tight.

"Daph, please. Let me just..."

His voice cracks. Tears are dripping down my face now. We're both soaking wet now. The rain gets heavier.

"Daphne, I love you."

These words! I've been waiting for since a month, but what's up with Gracia?

"Navon, why Gracia then?"

I ask.

He looks down, grabs both my hands and says,

"I've told her multiple times to stop clinging on to me. She wouldn't stop. Why do you think I told everyone we're dating? Because I want you all to myself. Daph, I'm sorry but I want you so bad. I Love you so much."

I don't say anything and I give him the tightest hug ever. He's resting his chin on the top of my head. I love you too I say under my breath I say as I'm still crying so much and as

I am holding on to. Navon I wanted you and now I have you for the rest of my life.

XVI

Chapter sixteen

" You got this Daph, I know you do."

I can hear Navon saying this over my headphones. I feel closer to father now. This feeling is just amazing it feels surreal.

"Land now."

I hear the trainer saying. I prepare myself and get ready for landing. Sooner and later, I manage a safe landing. Everyone applauds us as I come out of the plane.

"You did great, just like your previous landings."

Navon says as he gives me a hug. We go around the corner and get ready to go back home.

"Daph! That was actually phenomenal. Laast landing of the year was definitely yours."

Rider says.

"Thanks Rider."

"Anything to celebrate tonight?"

I look at Navon like, yeah I want to celebrate the last landing of the year.

"What do you say about a double date? You guys haven't met Raegan yet, haven't you guys?"

I smile because I love the idea. Want to see who this lucky girl is. But I also partially want to see if this Reagan is the girl that I used to hang out with. If Reagan is the girl who helped me get through my tough times. But yeah I do want to see her.

"Love that! Text me the address and we'll be there vy 7 if that's alright."

Navon says.

Rider smiles and he looks so damn excited. I can't believe it's been 6 months already since Navon and Daphne happened. Every day feels like a dream. Navon and I sit in the car and head home. Navan is driving.

"I'm so proud of you captain." Navon says. I smile at the word captain.

"Woah, we have an year left till we get 'pilot' so slow down buddy. But thank you. I am proud of you too."

I respond and Navon chuckles.

"By the way, have I ever mentioned about someone named Raegan before?" I ask.

"Riders girlfriend?"

"No, someone other than that."

Navon shakes his head as a no. Reagan was such a sweetheart to me. Sad I lost touch. Just riders girlfriend reminds me so much of her. We reach home and jump on our beds. Navon goes to his flat while I'm here. Honestly I'm not ready to move in together yet. It's a huge step which requires a lot of thinking. I don't feel like being lazy right now. To make something for Rider and Reagan. My specialty, brownies. Get up and head to the kitchen. I take all the ingredients out and start baking. Just then the doorbell rings. I go and open the door and see Navon smiling at me.

"Come in."

I say as I'm opening the door and rushing to the kitchen.

"Daphne it's 6:00 o'clock what are you doing."

Navon says as I am whisking the batter.

"Get the shape thingy you idiot!"

I scream. Navon starts laughing, but he gets it for me he puts it beside me and his hands slowly crawl up my waist as he slowly buries his face into the back of my neck. He gives my nape a slight kiss and rests his head on my shoulder. My stomach has a whole freaking zoo inside me I turn around and give him a hug.

"Put this in the oven, I'll go get ready."

I give him a peck on the cheek and rush to get ready after an hour i'm out all ready. I'm wearing a jute brown crocheted headband. I can already see the brownies packaged. I'm also wearing a white a line long dress with blue flowers on it.

"You look so damn cute."

Navon says.

"I appreciate the compliment, but it's 7, so let's go."

XVII

Chapter seventeen

"He's just coming in."

Navon says as we wait for Rider and Reagan. We are sitting down and I see them coming in. Navon and I get up. Reagan looks familiar I can't see until I see a close up of her. They start to walk more towards us and I can finally recognize her. Stop. Reagan! My childhood best friend! I can finally recognize her. Went to my eyes to see if it actually is her. It is! Her jaw drops.

"Daphne? Is that you?"

She says. I missed that voice so that much. I give her a big wide smile and the same way she gives me a hug. We are both squealing in excitement in a way that the whole restaurant is now scared of us. We pull back.

"Reagan! How've you been?"

I ask and we continue a conversation. I grab her arm and we walk towards the restroom, talking and leaving our men behind. Navon and Rider look at each other in confusion. After a few minutes Reagan and I come back we see Rider and Navon already stuffing their faces.

"Honest, What is wrong with the both of you." Reagan claims.

Reagan and I take a seat beside each other.

"So... How.. Do you guys.. know each other?"

Navon asks as he is chewing. I give him a look signaling him not to speak with food in his mouth. Sorry he mumbles under his breath.

"Sometimes I wonder if I'm his mother or girlfriend."

I say causing Rider and Reagan to laugh.

"We are childhood friends. We actually lost touch two years ago."

I say.

"Small world eh?" Rider says.

We enjoy the rest of our night and finally head towards the car. We say our goodbyes to each other and promise to keep in touch again. Navon sits in the driver's seat while I sit in the passenger seat. We take a sigh before starting the car.

"I had fun today, did you?"

Navon smiles and nods, but I can sense something is wrong with him. He is not acting himself.

"Babe, what happened?"

I ask facing him. Navon looks down at his hands fidgeting. A tear jobs in falls on his trousers I cup his face and make him face towards me.

"Tell me."

I give him a peck on the cheek.

"I miss mother. I just see mother in you. That's how I know you're the one."

I melt I didn't expect him to say that. I smiled and offer him my shoulders to cry on. He falls on to my shoulders and starts to sob. I pat his head and try my best to comfort him. I get this feeling but in a very different way. I just hope that his mother is in an amazing place right now. Honestly anywhere is better than Earth.

"It wasn't your fault. Never will be. She's in a better place right now." I whisper to him.

ꟈ

XVIII

Chapter eighteen

I place a flower on her grave and stand back. Navon then places another flower. I hold Navon's arm and caress it as I rest my head on his arm.

"Jewels Ruby. Father had despised that name."

I look at Navon as he says that. It's a beautiful name.

"Well, your father had bad taste but also reall good taste. I'm sure your mother was a gorgeous woman."

Navon chuckles on that.

"She was. She was one of the most beautiful woman I've ever witnessed. I just wish you could've met her."

Navon says. I really do want to meet her.

"Maybe I will. Not soon though."

Navon looks at me in confusion.

"In heaven."

I look at him and he smiles we look back at his mother take one final glance and finally walk towards the car. Silvia is holding the door open for us, we get in as Silvia drives. After an hour, we reach tò our flats. I spend the day at Navons flat. We're both on the sofa in front of the TV, trying to figure out what to do. I take the remote away from

Navons hand and put it down.

"Navon, what's on your mind?"

Navon is fidgeting with his fingers again. He looks at me and starts to cry again I hold him once again as he gets weak when he cries. He falls on to my shoulders and starts to sob.

"It's all my fault." His voice cracks."Forgive me mother, I love you."

And his voice cracks again.

I feel like crying with how much love he's showing his mother.

"It's not your fault. She loves you more."

Ohh God, please have her safe. I can't see Navon like this. Navon, your mother is really proud of you.

XIX

Chapter nineteen

FLASHBACK

JEWELS RUBY POV

Romain. The man I used to love back in high school is way different now. He always used to buy me my favorite flowers which are lilies. He always comforted me and made me feel loved after having Silvia and Navon. I don't know what happened now. He would hit me for every little thing to the point where I have bruises. So many bruises. His handprint on my back itched so much to the point where even with the slightest touch, it had bled. It grew purple and blue. I am casually sitting on my chair in front of the dressing table, doing my skin care. I am wearing my blue silk robe, the one which Romain always loved. Romain walks in and walks towards me.

"I told you not to wear this Robe ever again." He says as he places his phone on the dressing table beside me. My legs are shaking a lot. He doesn't do anything and leaves to use the restroom. Why shouldn't I wear this any more? What's wrong with it? He used to love it when I wore it. Just then his phone pings I looked to the side where his phone is placed. I ignore it but it keeps pinging. It's from trainer? His gym trainer? I open it and see the texts which read, 'when's our next session? last night was fun'.

I knew it. I knew he was cheating. I can't with him any more. I need to talk to him, now! He comes out of the restroom and I scream at him.

"ROMAIN!"

Romain flinches as he realizes what I have found. Romain runs towards me and I head back to the wall. He has his arm up against my neck. I try my best to get his arm out of my neck, but then he finally releases. At this point we are just screaming at each other. He bangs the door shut and leaves.

After a few minutes, I'm lying on the bed while I hear Navon and Romain discussing. I overhear them talking about getting the gun. Romain is disgusting for making his own son kill his mother. Navon is the smartest boy I've ever seen. I know he'll grow big someday. I lean my ear towards the bedroom door to hear what they're saying.

"'You'd do this if you love me Navon."

Even though Navon is the smartest boy I have ever seen. He would obey any one blindly because I have raised him that way. I have raised him in a way that he should never be able to disobey his elders. It's all right it's time for me to go. I cannot keep doing this anymore. I am going to complain to God about everything. I decide to write a letter, and when I do I place it where Navon can see it. I hop on to bed and pretend to sleep.

It's OK Navon. It's not your fault.

I hear footsteps. A gun loading in the bullets.

it's okay Navon, don't cry.

I hear the door opening.

It's all right, this is my time. I love you Navon, I love you Silvia.

END OF FLASHBACK

NAVON POV

I find a letter in the box as I'm organizing my stuff. I open it and look down only to see my mother's name. Mother wrote a letter for me I read the date and it's that day. I start to read.

' Dear Navon and Silvia,

This is your mother. I want to let you both know, I am sorry that I left without saying a word. Navon I'm so proud of you. For staying so strong during a matter and a situation like that. I swear, I am not mad at you. I am looking down at you from the clouds smiling. It's not your fault. Silvia you're my strong girl. I hope Navon is taking good care of you. I wanted the both of you to stick together no matter what. The both of you have made me so damn proud which made my life worth living. Let's meet ya? But before that, your life needs to be worth it. I believe in you guys. Your father was not a good person. It was only right for me to leave I love the both of you so much. You, Navon... Fly up high, right below me, close to me, I will say hi to you. Silvia,, make sure to make mother a design. For now, this is my goodbyes. But remember goodbyes are never permanent. We will meet. And remember I love the both of you so much. And I am really proud of you both. Right now as you are reading this I am having so much fun in heaven and I hope that you guys will make your life worth living and join up here with me. I'm waiting.

Love,

Jewels Ruby

Oh mother, how I miss you so much!

80

XX

Chapter twenty

BACK TO DAPHNES POV

"CHECK! Ladies and gentlemen, this is your captain speaking. Welcome to Canada Air plane please fasten your seatbelts as we prepare for takeoff. Hope you are comfortable throughout the flight. Thank you!"

I say and turn off my mic. I signaled my copilot to start. Something I've been waiting to do my entire life. Flying up high, right next to father this feels like a dream. I never want this dream to end. My first flight with actual passengers oh god! Just wait until I start my own airline I'm preparing for takeoff and so is my co pilot. After a few minutes I take off and realize I did it. This feels unreal. I call one of the air hostesses and ask,

"Call the passenger sitting in seat 35A, first class please."

The air hostess smiles and nods. A few seconds later, Navon reaches the cockpit.

"Hey captain!"

He says as he enters and takes a seat beside me.

"How're you feeling? First flight!"

How do I feel? I feel absolutely amazing. Like I can't describe this moment.

"I can't.. shit.. It all just feels like a dream. But there's so much more coming."

Navon gives a proud smile.

"I'm sure your father is really proud of you."

I smile. If only father was here to see me fly. There are so many people who depend on me. Their lives are in my hands right now. I need to be careful.

"When's your next flight?" I ask.

"Tomorrow. I need to fly to Italy."

Navon started flying way before me. I started today.

"I'll go now, there's only 2 more hours. I'm sleepy. Goodnight love."

He gives me a kiss on my forehead and leaves. Life is good I'm smiling so hard, I might even get the worst smile lines. Just then the air hostess rushes to the cockpit.

"Captain!"

She pants and pants.

"Its... passenger who sits at 35A. He has fainted!"

NAVON!? I rushed to the aisle and see him lying on the floor unconscious. I fall down to him holding him and I place his head on my lap. I slap his face a few times but no response.

"Someone get water!"

I scream at the top of my lungs. No one responds I go myself and get water. He was okay a few minutes ago. What happened? I grab a glass of water in my hand not too warm not too cold just the right temperature. I rushed towards him only to see him standing upright with the bouquet of pink roses.

What? Where? How? He's okay? He wasn't unconscious? What's going on? I catch my breath in relief that he is fine. I walk towards him crying and covering my face.

"Aww, it's okay, I'm okay."

He holds me onto his arms. I pull back.

"I was so worried! Idiot!"

I play fully hit him. And he laughs.

"Listen, I just want to say, I love you so much. The past few years has been a blast with you. I can't imagine a day without you I want to grow old with you and spend the rest of my life with you."

He's going to make me cry.

"So, I want to ask..."

He pauses. He hands me the bouquet and reaches for his back pocket. He starts to kneel down and open a box. It has the prettiest diamond ring ever. Oh my god, oh my God! This is happening in air!

"Will you fly with me for the rest of our lives by marrying me captain?"

Everyone isn't suspense of my answer. How can I say no? This really happened a thousand and more feet above ground.

"YES! YES! YES!"

I scream. He places the ring on my finger and gives me a hug. Everyone cheers and applauds for us. Navon I promise we will fly higher together.

XXI

Chapter twenty one

"Imagine people ask me who you are and I reply with 'my fiance'!"

I say as I blush so much and Navon laughs at my reaction. We are lying down on our hotel bed cramped up with each other. We are currently in Paris for a break until our next flight to Italy. Honestly, I want to start planning for my airline. It is a goal that I desperately want to achieve.

"Let's do something fun! Let's take a stroll through the Eiffel tower."

Navon suggests. I'm so down for it.

"I would love that." I get up and head to get ready.

After an hour or so, Navon and I Are wearing a white matching couple set. It is so cute. we head over to Eiffel Tower and reach in about 15 to 20 minutes.

"It's so beautiful."

I say looking at the Eiffel tower.

"Very beautiful indeed." He says. Not long later I realized he's looking at me. I look at him and smile as I realize he's saying that to me.

"I'm talking about the tower."

"I'm talking about my fiance."

I blush so hard my cheeks go red. We settle down in front of the Eiffel Tower on the grass.

"You know Daph, remember the first time we met and you talked about starting an airline."

I hum as a yes.

"I think we should start talking about it."

I badly want to so I nod as a yes.

"Let's start one together. I know we're serious about us."

I say.

Navon cracks a smile.

"I'd love that, it's been a dream for me too."

This movement is so precious to me which I am going to cherish until I die and after. Looking at Navon makes me feel like I have done a lot in my life. But still there is so much yet to achieve. I know I can do this when I have him by my side.

"Marcom White." He says.

I would love that considering it's named after father.

"I love it."

I say.

"Ladies and gentlemen, welcome to Marcom Air."

He says and tears form in my eyes. I love this and I cannot wait for this to happen.

"Hey, hey HEY! Idiot don't cry, Mr. White, look she's crying!"

Navon says as he looks up into the sky.

"She irritates me everyday. Give me tips on how to handle her... Haha, I agree Mr. White."

I hit him on his shoulder and we both laugh.
I hope you are the proudest father

XXII

Chapter twenty two

"Approved."

The chief says and ohh my God this rush of happiness flows in me. I jump onto Navon as he picks me up and twirls me around. He puts me down and we face the chief.

"Sorry... Thank you so much. I promise you will not regret this."

Navon reaches out for a handshake. As I reach my hand out the chief simply smiles and says,

"All the very best for Marcom Air, captain Daphne."

I mouth the words thank you and nod my head. We reach outside towards the exit of the cabin. I scream in excitement. This is an exciting, proud moment for Navon and I.

"Girl, we're still at headquarters."

Navon says. I can't hear anything. All I can think about is Marcom Air. I need to call Silvia and Reagan. I reach for my phone that is kept in the back pocket of my jeans. I texted them instead of calling them.

"We need to celebrate!" I exclaim.

Navon looks at me like he's excited.

"Let's go for bowling, we can then go for pizza."

He says.

I'm so excited that I can't wait. After an hour or two we reach the bowling alley where we meet Reagan and Silvia. It's the same place Reagan, Nora, Naomi and I used to go to all the time.

"I kinda miss California bowling alleys."

Reagan says.

I kind of do too but New York ones are heavenly amazing.

"Rea, do you remember how Nora, Naomi and us used to go here all the time when we were here? Those times were the best times even if it was for 6 months."

"I do miss them. It'd be so fun with them."

Navon and Silvia look at us confusingly.

"How many other people on Earth do you both know?"

Reagan and I laugh.

"Let's start shall we? I'll go register our names." Silvia says.

Silvia heads over to the counter. We look at the screens waiting to see what she would name us. It finally pops up and we see;

Captain Daphne, Captain Navon, CEO Reagan, CEO Silvia.

They are cute! First up is me. Everyone else is hooting as I get up and grab a ball in my hand. I wait to strike. I'm getting prepared as I hear a voice beside me. I stop and look beside.

"Hello Daphne."

It's Gracia. What is she doing here?

"Gracia? What're you doing in New york?" I ask.

She's bowling and strikes a six.

"I heard Navon is here, so I came."

It's time for me to humble this bitch up.

"So? Leave that. What have you been upto?"

I ask as she rolls her eyes. I can sense everyone at the pack biting their nails.

"Oh well, looking for a rich man. I don't have a job."

If all she did during training was go after men then obviously she doesn't have a job.

"Oh, good for you."

Gracia gives me a sarcastic smile.

"I heard Navon is single now. It's a shame you guys broke up and decided to be friends."

She's getting on my nerves. I can't deal with her right now.

"So, what have you been upto? Working in times square?"

I sigh in a sarcastic way like a scoff.

"First of all Gracia, Navon and I are engaged."

I pick up the ball, back up and prepare myself. I'm facing towards the pins as I say,

"Second of all, I'm very much pilot right now. I'm starting my own airline because I'm an independent woman who's never chased after guys during training."

She gives me a look. I turn back front and say,

"You'd never know because you failed. *Pause* Third of all *pause*"

I strike a six and I look at her in the eye.

"It's captain Daphne White."

She looks disturbed. But I am satisfied. I go back to the others and they give me this proud smile. I sit next to Navon and he pulls me closer to him by my waist and gives me a kiss on my forehead and whispers to me,

"Good job."

In a very deep voice. I look at Gracia and she stomps her feet out of the alley. She pushes the door open. As the door opens, Rider comes in. Gracia pushes him by the shoulder. Rider comes inside looking confused.

"YOO! Wasn't that Gracia?"

He comes in screaming. All of us laugh.

"Where the hell were you?"

Reagan says as she flicks his head. He grounds in pain rubbing his head with his palm. Reagan and Rider are really cute. We all laugh at that moment. This night is a core memory.

XXIII

Chapter twenty three

"Times square is so different now."

Reagan says. There is a lot of changes like more ads, more straight food places, There's more straight dances to now oh wow. This one street dance starts in front of me. I look and stop to watch. It is my favorite song. Everyone else stops. 5 minutes through the performance and this one dancer just catches my eye. She looks familiar. I squint my eyes only to say Nora! Oh my GOD! Nora Saffire! The girl with the most insane story. She was my girl. I can't believe she is here. What's up with me meeting almost everyone I know here especially in New York? I drag Reagan with a huge smile on my face.

" What's wrong with your face?"

Reagan says.

" Can't you see the dancer with the black crop top leather pants and black heel boots in the front? That's Nora. Nora Saffire!"

Reagan covers her mouth with her palm as she realizes. I turned to Reagan and my shoulder accidentally bumps into someone recording in front of me I apologize and they say,

" Its all right Daph."

HUH??? WHO IN THE HELL??

I turn to see who it is from the left and Reagan from the right we realize it's Naomi. Naomi Aster! What is going on! We squeal and give Naomi the biggest hug ever.

"What're you doing in New York?" I ask.

"I had an event to attend and I also came to visit Nora. She's doing really well for her self. What about you guys?"

"Captain Daphne." I say chuckling.

"Oh I know. I heard you're starting an airline. Congrats! Reagan, congrats on the company as well, maybe we can collab."

Naomi says. Word does spread fast so it's only reasonable she knows. We both thank her and Noras performance stops. Everyone is cheering and hooting like she is this famous celebrity. After two minutes, Her group settles and she walks towards us.

"OH MY GOD! REA? DAPH?"

Nora jumps on us and lets go of us finally.

" Sorry I'm quite sweaty."

We laugh.

" How have you guys been?" She asks. We have this small talk.

" I thought you wanted to be a cardiosurgeon, open up a hospital?"

Reagan asks.

"I am! Dr. Nora Saffire by day and Dancer Nora Saffire by night."

"What if you have surgeries within nights?"

"I have schedules Rea, don't worry, By the way congratulations on the airline and the company! Where's my invitation to the launch party?"

Nora Saffire. Still the same. Of course she is invited. I'm loving the way everyone's doing amazing for themselves

"Let's hangout today! Catch up on whatever we've missed out on. let's go to my place."

Nora says.

That's an amazing idea. We grab each others arms and start walking towards Noras car. I look back only to see Rider, Navon and Silvia so confused. I wave goodbye because right now it's me and my girls. We reached the car and get in. Nora is driving.

"Nora and Naomi, THE duo in high school. What have y'all been upto?"

Reagan asks.

"I have a crochet business, it's not much I mean it's fine."

Naomi says and Nora gasps.

"She's underexaggerating it, she's freaking CEO and makes around millions per day."

That's impressive! We praise her so much.

"What about you Nora?"

"Nothing much, like I said, dance, surgery."

Now Naomi gasps.

"You're underexaggerating it now, guys she has dance tour coming up, thats how she's famous. She has a hospital of her own and oh Lord she feels like my sugar mommy."

Naomi says and we all laugh. This is another core memory. Just then, Reagans phone rings and it's Rider. She picks up and clicks on speaker.

"Hon, atleast send me your live location so I know where you are."

"Okay I will, where are you guys?"

Reagan says.

"We're still at times square! You guys have the keys to the house."

We all laugh at the realization.

"Just wait until tomorrow, sleep on the streets."

Reagan says and hangs up. We laugh at the conversation.

XXIV

Chapter twenty four

"The tables should be closer to each other. The tablecloths are wrinkled! Start arranging the food!"

I'm stressing so much over this. I'm wearing a black Satin dress with a fur coat. I'm extremely worried that today might not go well. It's a very special day today. I take my phone out of my purse and go through the contacts. I can't do this without Navon. I'm walking as I look down on my phone I suddenly bump into someone in front of me and almost trip. They hold on to me on time. I look up only to see Navon.

"Woah chill Daph." He says.

"How can I chill? What if nothing goes well?"

He smiles.

"Why don't you go take some rest. I'll take care of everything. I'll call you when the guests arrive."

He says as he gives me a soft peck on my forehead. I smile knowing that I have won. I'm blessed with an amazing fiance. I walk my way towards the resting room. After an hour, I find myself greeting the guests. Rider and Reagan arrive wearing the sexiest set of black. I give them their name cards and their tables allotted. I see Nora and someone? It's a guy? Why is she holding on to him?

"Hey Nora."

She smiles and waves.

"This is Kai. My fiance."

From the inside, I am screaming, and pulling hair breaking glass. Nora always said she wouldn't date until she's achieved something. Can't believe she's stuck on to that. I signal her to tell me all about it later. She smiles and they head towards their table we are almost done with arranging the guests to their tables.

"I think that's all."

I claim and face backward to go inside.

" I think we have another special guest."

Navon says as he points. I turn around only to see Gracia. She is with this old man. She gives me this creepy sarcastic smile which I absolutely hate. First of all who the heck invited her?

"She's all yours."

Navon says as he rushes inside, leaving me to deal with her.

"Great to see you Gracia, but your name is not on the list. You and your father can leave."

Gracia gasps sarcastically,

"This is my fiance for your kind information."

I knew it.

"Sir, no offence, she's only with you for the money."

I say and shut the door close.

I giggle as I hear them arguing. I walk my way towards Nora and Reagan's table. I see Navon, Silvia and Rider standing there too. I rush into Navons arms as he holds me.

"It's almost time, we should go."

He says. i'm so nervous I might even puke.

" You guys got this!"

Rider says.

Others cheer for us. We're taking our seats and for some reason I feel really dizzy like everything around me is spinning, it's not good because I need to go up there on stage, take the blinds off of this huge model. It is shaped in an airplane. I can't wait to see what it is. I take a seat as Navon Sits beside me. I tap Navons shoulder and say, "I feel really dizzy."

He hands me a bottle of water and a bar of chocolate.

"Just captain things."

He says as he hands me the stuff. I smiled and immediately have it.

" Ladies and gentlemen may I have your attention please? Rider Flynn here."

Rider says on the mic and says his opening speech.

" Congratulations to Navon and Daphne. Can we have the both of you on stage and remove this blind off please?"

Everyone cheers and applauds as we walk up the stairs. I still feel a little dizzy but I hold onto Navon so I don't fall. Everyone is still cheering and hooting as we remove the blind. it's an airplane that says Marcom air. Everyone is cheering louder and louder. Looking at father's name on the airplane makes me feel like I've achieved so much in life. Everyone settles down for a bit as Rider hands the mic to Navon.

" I know that right now everyone has in their mind that I am going to speak but I feel like the right person to be speaking right now is Daphne."

Navon says and he hands the mic to me. I speak up,

" I honestly feel so overwhelmed. I can't even speak. This is a very special day for me and it's not me who was supposed to remove the curtains it was father."

I start to tear up and my voice starts to crack. Navon pats my shoulder and signals me that its okay.

" For those of you, who don't know my father passed away before I had even started training. The last thing he told me was a request. A request that I would fly high and be right under him near the clouds. He said the biggest thank you I could give him was by making him the proudest father. Right now in this moment I feel like I've made him more than just proud. When I was a kid he would tell me that if he ever dies early he would come for me for my proudest achievements as a butterfly and hit rest on my shoulder."

I start to cry.

" I'm still waiting on you father, thank you so much for giving me this opportunity. I love you father."

I put the mic away. As I do, I see a brown butterfly fly towards me and rest on my shoulder. That's how I know that father is here and he's looking at me. I start to breakdown. Everyone's cheering and applauding. The butterfly stays for some time and flies away. I immediately give Navon a hug on stage and start to cry and bawl my eyes out right there on stage. Navon and I get off stage and head to the restroom.

"You're amazing captain."

Navon says.

I feel dizzy to think about anything right now. I feel so light headed. My energy is going down. I fall onto Navons arms. I slowly close my eyes.

XXV

Chapter twenty five

I slowly flutter my eyes open. I can see Navon in front of me and an injection on my hand I am in an hospital gown lying down straight on the bed. I don't remember anything. The last thing I remember was giving a speech on stage.

"What's going on?" I ask Navon.

"You're fine. Let's wait for the doctor to get the reports."

Reports? Am I freaking dying!

After a minute or two, the doctor arrives. He comes inside the room with a nurse. Navon gets up and greets him. The dr greets him back. He grabs his glasses and inserts it in his shirt.

"Mr. White, I'd like to ask you something."

Mr?

"It's Ms. White, but yeah sure."

"Oh, I'm sorry, the last patient here was also a white. Years ago. Anyways, I'd like to ask if you've been feeling nauseous and sick lately?"

I nod as a yes.

"I don't know if this is good news or not, but she's pregnant."

Navons eyes widen and he cracks a huge smile on his face. My ears can't believe what they just heard. Definitely wasn't on the list to get pregnant before getting married but this is it. I feel so happy! I am happy. Just hope Navon is happy with this. This definitely wasn't our plan.

" I leave the both of you to be."

The doctor smiles and starts to walk away. He reaches the door and turns back,

"They're twins by the way."

He smiles and leaves. That's another shocker. I'm carrying two? Navon sits beside my bed with a huge smile on his face. He holds my head and says,

" Listen Daph, I know this was never on our list but imagine how amazing this will be. Our kids."

I smile.

" I'm not disappointed. I'm excited. I mean that's our kids! We can handle everything so don't worry Navon."

" I can't believe this, our kids... I promise we're going to be amazing daphne. You're gonna be an amazing mother."

" You are going to be an amazing father."

" Daphne can I scream I'm so excited right now."

I chuckle.

" Go to it outside in the Garden."

I say and he rushes outside. I see outside in the garden. He is screaming his lungs out. I see an old woman just standing there and looking at him scream his lungs out.

"I'M GOING TO BE A DAD!"

He screams.

" Ohh congratulations!"

The old woman says as she pats his head. That's it father. You're a grandpa now.

ꙮ

XXVI

Chapter twenty six

" Are you sure you'll come?"

Navon asks. I nod as a yes.

The both of us are on the way to the office to discuss about Marcom Air. But before that, we make a stop at Nora's house and have everyone gathered so we could reveal the good news. We're wearing the most formal clothing. I knock on the door and I hear a male voice.

"Who is it?"

They say.

His voice is so deep what the hell?

" It's Daphne?"

I see and he opens the door. It's Kai! Oh God he's so tall. He's wearing a tight black t-shirt gray sweatpants, thick black framed glasses and messy hair. Damn Nora Saffire.

"Nora! They're here!" He screams out to Nora. I can hear Nora's footsteps.

" Please come in and have a seat."

Kai says and his voice is so intimidating. Navon and I reach the couch and take a seat.

" You guys want something?"

We nod as a no. We're good thank you is what we say politely.

"This is such a nice penthouse you have here."

Navon says.

"Nora got it for our anniversary. Our dating anniversary."

Just then, Nora enters and so do the other girls. What were they doing!

" What's the good news!!"

Reagan says.

I adjusted for them to calm down they take a seat and hand them a box. They're very excitingly open the box and it's a scan of my belly.

"You're PREGNANT?"

Naomi screams.

"SINCE WHEN?" Reagan screams.

"WHAT!" Nora screams.

"I'M SO EXCITED!" Silvia says over call.

They're all squealing with joy and jump onto me. Nevon reveals that their twins and their jaws drop all the way to the Earth's crust. They're so happy that it's making me happy.

" Guys calm down I have another surprise for you guys."

I hand them each a tail box in which they open up and it pops out saying 'will you be my bridesmaid.'

Reagan starts to sob. I give each of them a hug. Then I turn to Silvia on call.

"Silvia, I want you to be my maid of honor."

She sends a text message saying it's an honor. I can't wait now.

ꟈ

XXVII

Chapter twenty seven

It is D day. I'm a month pregnant with twins, about to fly high in a huge airplane. Yes, our wedding is in an airplane. It's not just any airplane it's an airplane belonging to Marcom Air. I'm wearing a white dress. It's made of the finest pearls from Spain. They cost God knows how much.

"Ready Daph?"

Silvia asks.

"You look manly." I say.

Silvia is wearing a pink tuxedo. She looks masculine.

"Yeah well, my someone-special is coming too you know."

Silvia blushes as she says. I tease her for it.

"Who's the lucky guy? Or girl?"

"Girl. Lucky girl."

That's really cute. Just then everyone else barges in.

"It's time!"

Nora says.

I look down the aisle of the airplane. The airplane is actually so huge. At this moment, I miss Father so much. He will come to me.. I know it. I see Navon standing there waiting in his amazing black tuxedo. He looks really hot. Nora and Kai first walk followed by Reagan and Rider and Naomi and Oliver. Lastly, everyone stands up for when it's my turn. I'm walking alone. Crazy to think that only a few years ago I hated Navon just the thought of him wanted me to stab him and now I'm marrying him. He is staring up. He mouths beautiful and I smile. A butterfly comes and rests on my bouquet. I knew he'd come. I reached the end of the aisle and face Navon.

"I custom made the airplane for us."

Why is this the first thing that this dude says?

" Act mature brother." Rider says and I chuckle.

" Was that not romantic?"

I chuckle his cuteness.

"You look magnificently beautiful I can't wait for after the wedding."

" Slow down, I'm pregnant."

I say as I chuckle. Speeches start and it's Navons speech. He grabs the mic from rider and says,

" To Daphne White, the captain of my life. I promised we'd fly high together. You fulfilled it by saying yes. If you ask the before me if this day was expected, he'd say no. Daphne, I love you. to the clouds and on. I promise to be an amazing husband and an amazing father to our kids."

He places his hand on my belly.

"We'll grow old and wrinkly together and I promise at an amazing cost all you have to do is always fly with me. Forever."

That was the cutest.

" You may now kiss the bride."

Navon grabs me by my waist, Pulls me closer and dips his lips onto mine. Everyone is cheering and applauding. Navon, We will fly higher than this, I promise!

XXVIII

Chapter twenty eight

I'm at home while Navon is out busy with the meetings and stuff. I feel really tired so I'm at home, he gives me a text,

Navon: I‘m coming home in a few, missed you guys :)

Me: We can't wait to see you too. <3

We refers to the twins and I. I put the phone down on the side of the couch while I'm seated. I hold on to my belly and pat on it as I hum a song father used to sing to me. A few seconds later I hear a loud bang on the door. That's kind of weird. Navon said he wouldn't come until a few minutes.I take support from the couch and slowly get up. Maybe he has a surprise for me I say convincing myself. I‘m almost there I whispered to myself as I hear another loud bang. I looked through the hole only to say no one there. I still open the door thinking maybe there's something on the door mat. I opened the door and there's nothing and no one there. I heard back inside. Maybe they knocked on the wrong door. As I'm locking the door, the door slams open and someone comes inside and covers my mouth as my screams get muffled. They forcefully placed me on the chair. i'm screaming and whimpering as I cry for help. I need Navon. They are finally facing me. The people from the French unit. I thought we were done with this.

" Who the hell are you? Why are you here?"

I am screaming at him. I'm trying and struggling to get my hands untied.

"Where's Navon? That little snitch left the French unit.... For you?"

He laughs sarcastically.

" Why.. are you... here?"

" What did you think? Marrying your enemy would get you away from all of this? Nuh uh honey."

He says as he's removing his gloves. He grabs my chin and pulls it upwards until I'm facing him.

"Navon... is NOT HERE!"

I scream.

"Well, aren't you a beast?"

He chuckles to himself. He removes a knife from his pocket and starts to scrape it on the kitchen counter.

"Pretty sharp, eh?"

He says cleaning it with a cloth.

"What do you want?"

I scream.

He runs towards me and points the knife towards my belly.

"WHERE IS NAVON?" I flinch.

The front door opens.

"I'm here Motherfucker."

Navon is here Thank God.

I start to sob so much not knowing what to do. Navon and the dude are throwing hands at each other until Navon grabs the knife and stabs him on the neck. I gasp. I'm shaking. No.. NO! This can't be happening again. I'm breathing heavily. How will we deal with this. He rushes to me as he says me panicking.

"Hey, hey, hey, calm down, shh."

He cups my face.

"Breath Daph, nothings going to happen, I promise, he's under a unit. It will stay under a unit. Nothings going to happen to me as well, so don't worry. Now calm down."

I drowned into his arms and bawl my eyes out. I'm trusting you Navon. I love you so much.

XXIX

Chapter twenty nine

NAVON POV

" Who was that though that day?"

Daphne asks as we sitting in front of each other in the park.

"That was my cousin."

I respond.

Daphne takes a huge sigh.

" What did he want?"

" After marrying your enemy, they go after the enemy or something whose really precious."

I don't want to tell Daphne about the fact that they are after our kids. They wouldn't be safe from here on out. I feel really bad for making our kids go through this.

" So they are after the twins?"

She asks with sincere eyes. I don't want to say yes so I don't even look at her.

"So, they're after the twins?"

This time she asks in a more stern voice.

"Daph, listen..."

"SO, THEY'RE AFTER THE TWINS?"

There's fear in her voice. I can sense it.

"ANSWER THE QUESTION NAVON."

"Everything's going to be fine."

"DO YOU REALIZE HOW THIS WILL AFFECT THEIR ENTIRE LIFE?"

She screams and panis while I let her vent it all out.

"WE NEED TO THINK OF SOMETHING."

She grabs my arm and we walk towards our house. We get in we sit down on the dining table.

"Navon, I'm due in no time, we can't risk our childrens lives for this. Is there a solution?"

There is a solution but I really don't want to use the solution.

"Divorce, that's the only solution."

I can see the stress built up within Daphne.

"Daph, if you just listen to me."

Daphne finally sits down with her head rested on her palms.

"Obviously we're not going to Divorce. I love you too much and I'm not complaining. This happened with my grandfather. He married our enemy and years later, they attacked his wife. The timings match Daphne. We're not even under a unit anymore. There's nothing to worry about. If anything happens, we report to the police, just be alert."

I say and she calms herself down. I cup her face and give her a soft peck on her forehead.

"You're fine, I'm fine. The kids will be fine."

I say.

I rest my forehead on hers and caress her belly. I can feel Daphne's smile. Her smile is the warmest and feels like a warm hug on a cold night. I look back up at her.

"Let's go to bed. I'm here if anything happens."

She heads towards the bedroom. It's midnight and I hear footsteps. I check on Daphne and she's sleeping like a log. I have a glance at her once again and move towards the footsteps. I crack open the bedroom door only to see a figure of a person holding a gun. I turned the lights on and they shoot. The sound is so loud as to which Daphne is awake I immediately roll back into the bedroom and shut the door I can still hear gunshots.

"Navon, what's going on?"

Daphne wakes up. I am taking the gun out from the drawer.

"Daph, call the police."

Daphne immediately gets up and starts walking towards the landline in our bedroom. As she does I hear her scream,

"SHIT!"

I look at her as I'm holding onto the door.

"MY WATER BROKE!"

"I'll call the police, just sit down."

I seem calm but I'm not! I called the police, and they said they'll be here in 5 minutes.

"NAVON IT HURTS!"

"Just hang in there, ambulance is on their way."

The door is getting hard to push now.

"FREAKING OPEN NAVON!"

The guy screams. Just then the front door opens,

"This is the police! Put your hands up in the air!"

I can hear the guns falling and I immediately go to Daphne. She is groaning in pain. The police barges in.

"She's pregnant?"

I nod as a yes. They take her as the ambulance arrives. Oh God I hope they're ok. I can't process anything that's happening or anything that's happened. I fall to the ground crying and sobbing.

"Sir, are you hurt? Let's take you with your wife."

I'm too weak to respond anything and do anything. I follow the policies orders. I'm sitting in the ambulance as Daphne is groaning in pain.

"It's going to be okay Daphne. You got this!"

Oh Daphne, I swear this is the cost of us being together.

ꕤ

XXX

Chapter thirty

DAPHNE POV

"OH MY GOD! OH MY GOD! OH MY GOD!"

Reagan comes towards me as I'm in the hospital bed.

"Are you okay? Are you good?" Rider asks.

I smile and nod. Just glad it's all over now. I'm glad Navon was there for me. This proves how much he loves me.

"Navon? Are you okay?" Nora asks.

Navon smiles and nods as well.

"The twins are beautiful."

Naomi says as she's holding on to them. Everyone else gathers her and admires the Twins. Naomi hands them to me and Navon. I look at Navon with teary eyes.

"Navon, our kids."

"Our kids Daph."

I kiss the both of them on the cheek.

"What have you guys named them?"

Rider asks.

"The girl is Jewels Ruby. Jewels Ruby Vanchover."

I say and Navon looks at me.

"I love it so much. Mother is going to be so proud of me."

He says.

"Jewels Ruby Vanchover and Mosco Vanchover."

I love the name so much. Everyone else leaves, leaving me and the Twins and Navon together.

"Navon, this is it. We made it."

"like I always said we would."

He gives me a kiss on the cheek.

"This doesn't feel real."

I say.

"I'm ready to fly higher with you love."

Navon And I started off as literal enemies. I can't believe all of this has happened. This all feels so unreal. It feels like this once in a lifetime memory. All happening at once. Navon And I promised each other that we'd fly high. I can't believe we're more than just flying high. I can't believe this. Sooner or later we'd reach the stars together, but this time with our moons.

"I promise to protect the both for the rest of your lives."

I say to the Twins while holding on to them. Father, you're a grandpa now. I hope you're proud of me. Thank you so much father. Thank you so much Navon.

"You've made our parents their grandchildren Daph. I'm so proud of you."

I smile. This was the cost of which Navon was talking about. A cost which was so worth it. A cost which comes all under the act of killing. Let's fly high he said, I'm ready to fly till the stars and beyond.

www.ingramcontent.com/pod-product-compliance
Lightning Source LLC
La Vergne TN
LVHW091032150826
845672LV00006BA/1778